Selkie

GILLIAN McCLURE

FARRAR, STRAUS AND GIROUX

NEW YORK

Far away, on the edge of the sea, a boy named Peter lived with his granny. At high tide, the sea stretched from their cottage to Seal Island. But at low tide, the sea drew back and uncovered a long stretch of sand.

"Stay away from Seal Island," Peter's granny said.

But the cries of the seals on the wind kept calling Peter.

"I want to go to Seal Island," said Peter.

"It's too dangerous," said Granny.

"I can walk across the sands when the tide is out."

"The sands are dangerous," said Granny. "They are soft in places, and will suck you in if you don't tread carefully."

"But the oysterman knows a safe way across the sands," said Peter. "He has oyster beds on Seal Island."

"Stay away from the oysterman," said Granny. "Don't try to follow him."

At low tide, Peter continued to watch the oysterman go carefully over the sands, leaving a line of sticks to mark his way.

Before high tide, the oysterman returned with a sackful of oysters to sell. Peter watched him lifting his sticks, one by one, with the sea coming in behind him.

One day, when Granny was not looking, Peter ran to
the cottage where the oysterman lived with his wife.
Peter found him outside, mending nets and chanting:

"One day I'll catch a selkie—
a selkie who will help me
learn the language of the sea.
One day I'll catch a selkie—
a selkie who will help me
gather riches from the sea!"

"Please, Mr. Oysterman," said Peter, "will you show me the way over the sands to Seal Island?"

The oysterman jumped up and roared, "Stay away from Seal Island, boy!" and threw his net at Peter, but only caught Peter's hat.

Peter ran back to his granny.

Granny was angry. "Next time, it won't just be your hat caught in the oysterman's net."

"He wants to catch a selkie," Peter said. "What's a selkie, Granny?"

"A selkie is a seal that turns into a girl when she takes her sealskin off," Granny replied.

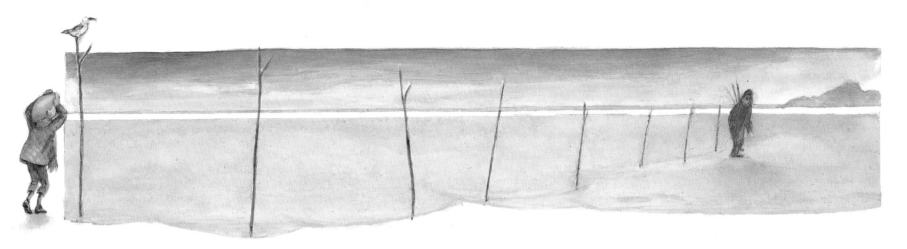

The next day, Peter slipped out to look for his hat.

It was low tide, and he saw the oysterman far out on the sands on his way to Seal Island. The path of sticks started from the oysterman's cottage.

Peter thought, "If I follow the sticks, then I can teach myself the safe way over the sands." He set out carefully.

When he reached Seal Island, Peter saw the oysterman bent over his oyster beds. Peter went around to the other side of the island and came upon a flock of seals on the rocks. Suddenly Peter heard splashing coming from a pool.

Peter saw a beautiful seal caught in
one of the oysterman's nets.

As he struggled to free the seal, her skin slipped off and a young girl stood there.

Peter gasped, "You must be a selkie!"

The girl smiled at him. "Yes, I am," she said. "How can I thank you for setting me free?"

But before he could reply, Peter felt the sea lap over the top of his boot.

"The tide's coming in!" he cried. "Quick! I must cross the sands while the oysterman's sticks are still there."

When he ran to the other side of the island, he saw the sea
stretching over the sands and, in the distance, the oysterman
lifting his last stick.

"You must stay on Seal Island until the tide goes out again," said Selkie.

Peter knew he had hours to wait and that his granny would be worried.

"Dear friend," said Selkie, "you set me free and now I will begin to teach you the secret language of the sea."

She taught Peter to hear the voices of the fish, to see the patterns of the waves, and to know the words of the wind.

The hours went by, and soon the tide began going out again.

Peter told Selkie, "The oysterman thinks that learning the language of the sea will make him rich."

Selkie said, "A greedy man can never learn the language of the sea. He is only listening for the jingle of coins."

They laughed together and never noticed that the sea had drawn completely back, uncovering the way over the sands from Seal Island.

Suddenly there was the oysterman with his net.

"Got you!"

Selkie tried to put on her sealskin and escape, but the oysterman grabbed the skin with one hand and held the net firmly over Selkie with the other.

As the oysterman dragged Selkie
over the sands, Peter heard his chant:

"*Today I caught you, Selkie.*
I will make you help me
learn the language of the sea.
Today I caught you, Selkie.
I will make you help me
gather riches from the sea."

Peter followed the oysterman ashore.

The oysterman took Selkie into his cottage
to show his wife. Peter crept close and peered
through the window.

He saw the oysterman's wife dressing Selkie
in an old petticoat.

When Peter got home, his granny sent him straight to bed. But he couldn't sleep.

He was worried about Selkie. He had to help her get back to Seal Island, and he was trying to remember the pattern of the sticks in the sand.

Selkie could not sleep, either. The seals were calling her. She saw the sea stretching out to the island, but she knew she could not swim there without her sealskin. Later she saw the sands stretching out to the island, but she knew she could not walk there without the oysterman's sticks to guide her.

The next day, Peter went to the oysterman's cottage. He saw him loading his cart with oysters to sell. He heard him grumbling about his lazy wife, who never got up in the mornings.

Peter knew he would be gone all day.

Inside the cottage, Selkie sat weeping. A bowl of porridge the oysterman had given her was untouched.

In her bed, the oysterman's wife snored.

Peter crept in. "Quick! Follow me across the sands to Seal Island while the tide is out. I've remembered the way."

"But my sealskin," sobbed Selkie. "I cannot swim with the seals without it."

They searched everywhere in the cottage. It was nowhere to be found. Just as they were about to give up, Peter looked up in the rafters.

And there he found the sealskin!

Taking the oysterman's sticks and placing them in the pattern he remembered, Peter led the way safely over the sands.

When they reached the island, Peter turned to Selkie, but she had already put on her sealskin. Instead of a girl, a beautiful seal was sliding down to the water's edge.

As she dove in, Peter heard her call out goodbye to him in the language of the sea.

Peter felt sad. For a long time he watched Selkie swimming with the seals.

By the time Peter turned to go back, darkness was falling. The tide was coming in fast. He saw a light moving along the far shore. It was the oysterman returning home. Peter set off.

The sea swirled around his ankles, then his knees, then his chest. But he was not afraid, because the patterns of the waves, the voices of the fish, and the words of the wind led him safely back to shore.

As Peter came out of the water, he saw
the oysterman raging outside his cottage:

"You've freed my precious Selkie!
Now I can't make her help me
gather riches from the sea!"

Then Peter shouted,

"Dear Selkie, you have taught me:
better than all its riches
is the secret language of the sea."

As the wind carried Peter's cry out to sea, a
seal's head slipped silently under the waves.

Color separations by Bright Arts, Hong Kong
Printed in Singapore by Tien Wah Press
First published in England by Doubleday,
a division of Transworld Publishers Ltd, 1999
First American edition, 1999

Library of Congress Cataloging-in-Publication Data
McClure, Gillian.
 Selkie / Gillian McClure. — 1st American ed.
  p.   cm.
 Summary: When a greedy oysterman captures a selkie, a seal that turns
into a girl, a boy outwits him and returns her to the sea and wins her reward.
 ISBN 0-374-36709-4
 [1. Selkies—Fiction.   2. Seals (Animals)—Fiction.   3. Islands—Fiction.]
I. Title.
PZ7.M4784141945Sg   1999
[E]—DC21   98-55143